To Ivo — *JW*

To my biggest beloved
kisser, Luca — *JA*

SIMON AND SCHUSTER
First published in Great Britain in 2010 by Simon and Schuster UK Ltd
1st Floor, 222 Gray's Inn Road, London WC1X 8HB
A CBS Company

Text copyright © 2010 Joanna Walsh
Illustrations copyright © 2010 Giuditta Gaviraghi

ISBN: 978-1-84738-435-5 (HB)
ISBN: 978-1-84738-436-2 (PB)
Printed in China
2 4 6 8 10 9 7 5 3 1

The Biggest Kiss

Joanna Walsh & Judi Abbot

SIMON AND SCHUSTER
London   New York   Sydney

Kisses on noses,

kisses on toes-es.

Sudden **kisses** when you least supposes.

Who likes to **kiss**?

I do!   I do!   Even the shy do.

Why not try, too?

Frogs like to **kiss,**

and dogs like to **kiss.**

'normous

elephants do.

Little tiny ants do.

Do worms **kiss** underground, with the soil all around?

Do fish **kiss**
like this —

splosh,

splash,

splish?

Some **kisses** are misses,
they land on the ear or near.

But **kisses** with lipstick stick like . .

a **kiss** with honey,

a **kiss** that's yummy,

a **kiss** on the elbow,

a **kiss** on the tummy.

The rain's **kiss** on your skin is fun.

The snow's **kiss** on your face is ace.

The
TALLEST
kiss is a
tricky kind.

The smallest **kiss** is hard to find.

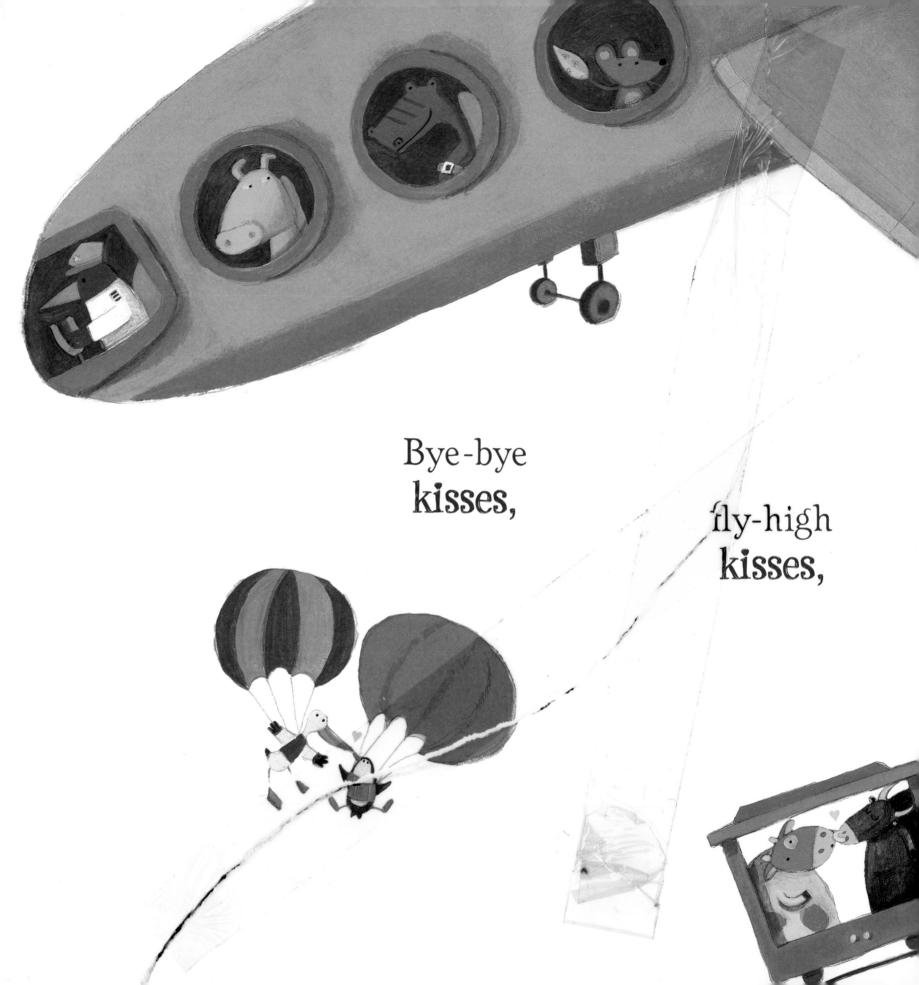

Bye-bye
kisses,

fly-high
kisses,

eye-dry
kisses,

all my
kisses.

I wish for a **kiss** before breakfast,
to start the day right.

And a **kiss** at the end
to say, "Good night!"

I've had all these **kisses**,
and lots more too.

But the very
best kiss . . . .

is a **kiss** from you!